TIME TWISTERS

TIME AND SPACE

Calico

An Imprint of Magic Wagon
abdopublishing.com

BY KATHRYN LAY   ILLUSTRATED BY DAVE BARDIN

FOR RICHARD AND ALL OUR ADVENTURES PAST AND FUTURE. —KL

FOR MY MOM, WHO GAVE ME MY FIRST SKETCHBOOK AND HAS NEVER STOPPED GIVING. —DB

abdopublishing.com

Published by Magic Wagon, a division of ABDO, PO Box 398166,
Minneapolis, Minnesota 55439. Copyright © 2017 by Abdo Consulting
Group, Inc. International copyrights reserved in all countries. No part of
this book may be reproduced in any form without written permission from
the publisher. Calico™ is a trademark and logo of Magic Wagon.

Printed in the United States of America, North Mankato, Minnesota.
102016
012017

THIS BOOK CONTAINS
RECYCLED MATERIALS

Written by Kathryn Lay
Illustrated by Dave Bardin
Edited by Tamara L. Britton & Megan M. Gunderson
Designed by Laura Mitchell

Publisher's Cataloging-in-Publication Data

Names: Lay, Kathryn, author. | Bardin, Dave, illustrator.
Title: Time and space / by Kathryn Lay ; illustrated by Dave Bardin.
Description: Minneapolis, MN : Magic Wagon, 2017. | Series: Time
    twisters ; Book 1
Summary: Luis, Tyler, Casey, and robot cat Steel discover Tesla's Time
    Twister, a time machine, and journey into the future where they face
    aliens, an evil robot, and a spaceship in distress, and try to help
    Uncle Cyrus who is stuck in time.
Identifiers: LCCN 2016947756 | ISBN 9781624021770 (lib. bdg.) |
    ISBN 9781624022371 (ebook) | ISBN 9781624022678 (Read-to-me
    ebook)
Subjects: LCSH: Time travel--Juvenile fiction. | Best friends--Juvenile
    fiction. | Space ships--Juvenile fiction. | Adventure and adventurers--
    Juvenile fiction. | Survival--Juvenile fiction.
Classification: DDC [Fic]--dc23
LC record available at http://lccn.loc.gov/2016947756

TABLE

OF

CONTENTS

CHAPTER ONE

THE TREE-SHAPED KEY

Luis stood at the top of the stairs and imagined he was Indiana Jones at the edge of a cliff, being chased by men with spears. The doorbell rang. It must be his rescuers.

Luis ran down the stairs two steps at a time. His mom would've yelled at him for it. But she was away all week in Puerto Rico taking care of her sick mother.

"I'll get it!" he shouted when the doorbell rang again.

Luis skidded across the floor. He yanked the front door open to see his two best friends, Tyler and Casey Jenson.

Luis gasped, "I'm being chased by the bad guys! Thank goodness you're here!"

Tyler laughed. "It's about time you answered the door. We have something incredible to tell you." He pushed Luis aside, nearly knocking him over with his crutches.

"Watch it, or I'll turn those into skates," Luis said. He was about to shut the door when something ran into his foot.

MEORR . . . BOING!

Luis bent down and picked up Tyler's robotic cat. Tyler had spent six months building the sleek silver creature at the college science lab where his father worked. He was filled with sensors and computerized parts. The cat still had some problems, but Tyler kept improving his project.

"Hey, what's wrong with Steel?" Luis asked.

Tyler shrugged. "Something in his voice box got corrupted when Mr. Davidson's bulldog knocked him over."

Luis closed the door behind them. It was the first day of spring vacation and he planned to spend the whole week with his two best friends. They would argue about what to do, but each of them would take turns choosing. And whatever it was, it would definitely be adventurous.

"So, what do we do first?" Luis asked. "Go to the library for some old adventure videos? Go to the museum so Tyler can see that new robot exhibit? Or head to the junk shop for some weird gadgets for Casey to put together?"

Tyler bent down and whispered something into Steel's pointed ears.

Luis had known right away when Tyler showed up at school last year that they would be friends. Luis loved astronomy, and Tyler had stars and planets painted on his crutches.

Tyler stood. "Pick him up. He has a new command."

Steel pushed his head forward and stuck out a silver tongue and flicked it against Luis's cheek.

"It's cold," Luis said. "And stiff."

Casey shoved her brother away. "Who cares about your old cat? We have something more interesting to show you, Luis."

She unzipped a pocket on her jacket. Her gray jacket was covered with buttoned and zippered pockets that held tools she could use to take apart and build things. It reminded Luis of a magician's suit, full of surprises. She reached into the pocket and said, "Hold out your hand."

Luis was never sure what to expect from Casey. A key fell into his hand. It was long and shone like real gold. The top of the key looked like a tree with branches twisting around it.

"Wow, what is it?" Luis asked.

Tyler grabbed it from his Luis's hand. "We found it in Dad's office. We think it's the key for your father's shed."

"You swiped it?" Luis asked.

Casey put her hand over Luis's mouth. "Quiet! We don't want your father to hear. We, uh . . . accidentally found it. We were looking for this special tool Tyler uses on that cat of his. This key was in a box under the little toolbox."

Luis had promised his dad a million times to stay away from the shed in the back field beyond the edge of their long backyard. But sometimes when their fathers were working inside, Luis and his friends would listen against the metal door.

They had heard strange noises and angry yells. Once, the whole building seemed to glow. When they heard crackling, electrical noises and what sounded like an explosion, they ran away and didn't go back for a week.

Luis's dad walked into the hall, his car keys jangling in his hand. "You kids have exciting plans for the week?"

"Yes, Mr. Sanchez," Tyler said. "Very."

Luis's dad nodded. "Good. I'm on my way to meet your father at the university library. Luis, if your mom calls, ask her how Grandma is doing and when she's coming home." He peered over his glasses at them. "Stay away from the shed."

Luis groaned. His dad told them that every single day.

They stood by the window and watched until he drove his car away.

"Our dads will be gone all morning," Tyler said. "It's the perfect chance to see what's going on in that shed."

Luis said, "But we're not allowed."

"We won't touch anything," Casey promised. "We just want to see what the big secret is inside. Aren't you dying to know? They've been working out there ever since that big crate came to your house."

Luis nodded. Of course he was curious about it. More than curious. Maybe it wouldn't hurt if they just had a peek inside.

"Come on, Luis," Casey pleaded. "An engineer and a science professor spend hours every day in a huge, locked shed? It has to be something amazing."

Luis grinned. "Okay," he said.

He grabbed Steel and followed Casey and Tyler outside. They ran around the house to the backyard and slipped through an opening in the fence between the yard and the shed.

Two weeks ago, a huge, mysterious crate had been delivered on a flatbed truck. It came from the estate of Luis's great-great-great-great-uncle Cyrus, a relative they'd never even heard of before then.

There was a letter with it. But all Luis's father would tell him and his mother was that this long-ago mysterious uncle had disappeared in the late 1800s. The crate, along with a suitcase of personal items, had been locked away in the basement of an old house and discovered when someone new bought the house. The closest living relative they could find was Luis's father.

The next day, workers arrived and put up a large metal shed and moved the crate inside.

Luis and his friends stopped at the tall door. Luis tugged at the large lock. They'd tried picking it once, but it gave Casey an electric shock.

Luis held out the key. They were going to be grounded all week if their fathers found out they had been inside. Maybe for the rest of the year.

Casey said, "Why are you waiting?"

Luis didn't answer. There could be an amazing adventure inside, better than all his imaginings. Or it could be full of boring, dusty antiques.

Casey grabbed the key from him. She stalked up to the door, took a deep breath, and pushed the key into the lock.

At first, nothing happened. She shook it, then turned it the other direction.

Sparks flew from the lock, but she didn't get shocked. The lock shook and rattled until it fell open with a puff of smoke and a loud *whoosh!*

"Wow," Tyler said.

Luis put the lock and key in his pocket. He pulled hard on the door until it swung open.

The shed was dark. Luis pulled his cell phone from his pocket and turned on its flashlight. The small light was just enough for him to find a light switch nearby.

He flicked it on and heard his friends gasp.

"Look at all this stuff!" Casey said. She practically danced into the room.

Luis groaned. Casey might as well be in a candy store. They'd never get her to leave. Casey loved to take apart and rebuild electronics and things that worked with batteries and levers and wheels. Metal parts and pieces covered tables on one side of the room. Casey moved toward them as if pulled by a magnet.

"Don't touch anything!" Luis yelled.

Casey put her hands behind her back and walked along the tables.

But Luis could see her fingers twitching. Then he heard a metallic sound.

MEOWFFF! BOING!

"Hey, come here," Tyler shouted. "Steel found something."

Luis looked where Tyler pointed. Steps led up to something very tall and wide standing on a wooden platform. A green tarp covered it.

Casey ran up onto the platform. "This is what our dads are working on?" She waved her arms. "It's humongous!"

Luis hurried up the stairs. He grabbed the bottom of the tarp and tugged. It moved only a little. "Help me!" he said.

Tyler leaned on his crutches and Casey held onto the tarp near Luis's hands.

"Pull!" Luis shouted.

They tugged and grunted until Luis was sure his arms would fall off.

"Pull harder!" he yelled.

They toppled back as the tarp fell around them. Steel meowed and wheeled out from under it. His green eyes glowed.

Tyler whistled to Steel. The robot moved to his side. Steel grabbed the edge of one of Tyler's crutches, which had fallen. Steel's legs stretched and raised his body until Tyler grabbed the crutch and put his hand back through the handle.

Luis stared at the metal object on the platform. Glass walls surrounded a narrow steel door, held together by copper colored metal.

The glass shone like a mirror. It showed nothing of what was inside. Tall, thick wires came out of the top corners, meeting and twisting up through a hole in the shed's roof.

Tyler walked up to the box and rubbed his hand on it. He reached as high as he could, still not reaching the top. "It's like a rocket ship without engines. Or some kind of magician's box. Or . . ."

YANK!

Luis tapped the glass. It was thick and barely made a sound. The metal frame had huge silver bolts holding it together. He pressed his face against the glass but saw only his reflection.

"Maybe it's some kind of transporter?" Luis asked.

"Maybe it's some kind of clone box," Tyler suggested. "Our dads would be famous! They could feed the world with cloned food or something."

Casey gasped. Luis turned toward her.

She pointed to an old-looking plaque on the side of the machine.

"I know what it is. I know what it is!" she said.

Luis leaned forward and read the words on the plaque.

TESLA'S TIME TWISTER

CHAPTER TWO

THE TIME TWISTER

The three friends stared at the machine.

Casey looked Luis in the eyes. "Our dads are working on time travel?"

Luis stepped back from the metal machine. "This must be a joke. Don't you think it's just a joke?" he asked, his voice coming out like a squeak.

Casey laughed. "Our dads don't joke about stuff. I mean, they are serious scientific brains. But I didn't think they were this smart."

Luis knew she was right. Their fathers were serious when it came to science. But if this was real, why didn't their fathers tell them about it? How could they keep such a secret from their kids?

"Our dads are seriously cool," Tyler said, walking up to the machine.

"Don't touch anything, remember?" Luis said.

Casey folded her arms. "Seriously? You want to look inside as bad as we do."

They all stared at one another a moment.

"Okay," Luis said.

"Okay. Let's figure out a way inside," Casey said. She pushed her hand against a rectangle where the door handle should have been. "Oh," she said. "Something clicked under my fingers."

They leaned close as a small panel opened up. A tiny keypad glowed red.

"It must use a code to open," Tyler said. He pushed on the numbers.

Casey shoved his hand away. "Stop it, before you set off some kind of alarm. We have to think this through. There are three double-digit spots there."

Luis nodded. Casey loved to figure things out. Puzzles and the ends of movies and video games where you had to think about the next step.

Casey tapped her finger against her cheek. "What would our dads use as a pass code? Numbers are harder than a word. Three two-digit numbers. Hmmm."

Tyler said, "There are three of us."

Casey slapped him on the shoulder. "Brilliant, big brother! So what are the numbers? Months we were born? Days of the month? Last two numbers of the year?"

She tried each of their numbers, but nothing happened.

"What about our ages?" Tyler suggested.

Casey snorted. "That would be dumb. We're all the same age."

Luis shrugged. "Try it."

Casey tapped 1-0-1-0-1-0.

Without a sound, the metal door slid into one of the glass panels.

They peeked inside. The room was small, but there were four chairs against one side. The rest of the room was empty except for one large panel full of switches and levers in front of the first two chairs.

"What's this?" Tyler asked. He picked up something from one of the chairs. He held out a small red notebook. A thick rubber band held it shut. Tyler held it out to Luis.

"You open it," Tyler said.

Luis took the notebook. It looked old. Really old. He slowly removed the rubber band. The book fell open. Yellowed pages were filled with scribbling. It wasn't his dad's handwriting.

"What does it say?" Tyler asked, standing on his toes to peer over Luis's shoulder.

Luis turned the first page. There were strange-looking diagrams of the machine. Three pages were filled with drawings and mathematical calculations around the diagrams.

Small, inked writing began on the fourth page.

We believe we have hit on the secret at last. I did not accept it at first, but it truly appears as if the machine may actually be working. Tesla has not slept in days. He does nothing but work on the machine. He eats little, mumbles a lot, and shouts at me more than I like.

Luis stared at the words he had read. The journal had to have belonged to his great-great-great-great-uncle Cyrus.

"This belonged to Cyrus, I just know it," Luis said. "But who was this Tesla guy?"

Tyler groaned. "Nikola Tesla, the famous scientist and inventor? He was better than

Thomas Edison. Don't you read anything besides adventure books?"

Luis shrugged. "Sometimes." His heart beat faster. A real time machine? Like H.G. Wells wrote about? If his uncle and this Tesla guy created the machine, why had no one heard of it before? Had they used it? He'd give anything to be able to read about their adventures if they had made it work.

He glanced through the journal. It had more numbers and symbols. There were notes about how much steel they bought and the weight of the machine.

"Did they go anywhere in it?" Tyler asked. "Did it even work?"

Luis looked at the last few entries in the journal. He cleared his throat and read.

Although the machine seems to be in working order and we have sent many small animals through who have returned unharmed, it is only through man that we can learn whether the machine has truly traveled in time. So, Tesla brought in his favorite Labrador, Socrates, the chocolate one with the droopy ears. We trained Socrates to leave the machine and return to it. We even taught him to open and close the door in case that was necessary upon arrival.

"Poor dog," Casey said.

Luis waved a hand at her. He read more.

Tesla put Socrates into the machine. I set the time for two years from today. A note was pinned to the dog's collar instructing whoever found him to tuck a newspaper into it. The machine was set for the door to open on arrival of the time he had set. We hoped the dog would come back to us on the return date, which was set for 24 hours later.

Luis wondered if they were afraid for the dog. It might never come back. Someone might find him and just keep him. He read on.

We sat by the machine for twenty-four hours, only one another and a bit of food and water for company. When the time was up, the machine whirred and smoked. It had brought something back. The door opened, and Tesla's dog leapt out at us. I grabbed for the paper that had been pushed into his collar.

Casey leaned over Luis's shoulder and read.

Success! The date was two years from now. We were looking at news from the future. Tesla immediately grabbed the paper and threw it into a nearby fire. Why had he created the machine if he was so fearful of the future? Tomorrow, one of us will test the machine. I am both fearful and excited.

Luis closed the book. "That's all there is."

Casey grabbed her brother by the arm. "It worked. It really worked."

Tyler grinned. "I wonder if our dads have tried it yet."

Luis pointed at a section on the control panel. There were two dials. One could be set for months and the other for years. There was a large lever labeled *Advance* under them.

"It's amazing. It's crazy," Tyler said. His fingers hovered over the dates.

"Hey, what are you doing?" Luis shouted.

"We should go for a spin," Tyler said. "Just a short one and back. We could see what kind of pop quiz Mrs. Sharp is giving on Friday so we could study for it. Or we could go two weeks ahead and find out what parts we're getting in the school play."

Casey nodded. "Or we could go to last Thursday and see who stole my bike wheels."

Tyler said, "That's not very exciting. How about a real adventure."

"An adventure?" Luis said. "It's going to be a big adventure when our dads catch us here."

Steel butted its head against Casey's leg. "Or, we could just send Steel," she said.

Tyler grabbed Steel. Its metallic legs kept moving. "You aren't sending my cat out alone."

"Okay, okay." Luis knew Tyler and Casey were as excited about the idea of testing it as he was. Tyler was a bit wild, but he loved anything to do with science. He wanted to be either an astronaut or a robot builder with his dad. And Casey was so smart she learned something new every month. Playing guitar, scuba diving, building a go-kart engine.

Casey took the journal and looked through the pages. "How do you think it works?"

Luis waved his hands over the dials. "I guess you just set the date you want to go to and push the green button. I bet the machine does the rest."

Casey moved the date to two weeks in the future. She grinned at them. "I've never acted in a play before. I tried out for the lead. I'd make a cool Robin Hood. Let's just find out if I got it."

Luis saw a button that showed a picture of a door. He pressed it and the door slid back into place. It all seemed so old-fashioned and futuristic at the same time.

"Okay, strap yourselves into a seat," Casey ordered. "Luis, sit on the end and then you can lean over and hit the button. It was your uncle who helped build it, after all."

Luis snapped the straps across his chest. He reached for the button. He could just touch it with the edge of his finger.

"Three . . . two . . . one!" Tyler shouted.

Luis took a deep breath and stretched his arm a little further. As he pressed the button, a siren went off. He yelled and yanked his arm back.

That's when he knocked his elbow against the lever labeled *Advance*. The date dials spun fast. Very fast. Months and years clicked by.

"Uh-oh!" Luis shouted.

Tyler's eyes went wide. "Uh-oh? What does that mean?"

Luis felt the machine spin. Faster and faster. It felt like it must feel to be inside a tornado.

Luis tried to reach the Advance lever, but his arms were pressed against his sides. The machine twisted back and forth. He tried warning his friends that they were moving fast through time, but his lips felt like they were glued together.

Luis's whole body shook. Then a blinding light filled the machine. His friends' bodies seemed to twist like pretzels. Luis felt sick to his stomach as his own body twisted.

Then Luis was surrounded by a gray cloud.

He forced his mouth open and screamed. And the twisting feeling disappeared.

Luis couldn't see the time machine. He couldn't see his friends. He closed his eyes. Had they gone to the end of time? Was he alone?

When he opened his eyes again, the cloud was gone. He was sitting at a large control panel. There were people all around. They were talking. Machines were beeping. Luis turned to see Tyler and Casey seated next to him.

"Captain, are you okay?" a voice asked.

Luis blinked. A man in a metallic green jumpsuit stood behind Tyler.

What happened to the time machine? Where were they?

"What?" Luis asked.

"We've been given the all clear. We can go to docking speed, sir."

"Docking speed?" Luis asked.

"We've arrived at the space station, sir."

Luis looked at the large screen in front of them. It was showing a film with stars and a long white object in the middle.

Luis blinked. It wasn't a film. Or a screen. It was a window.

Luis looked at his friends. They stared back with wide eyes. This wasn't Wilton Elementary. They weren't watching Casey's play rehearsal.

They were on a ship going through space.

And he was the captain.

CAPTAIN SANCHEZ

Luis stared at the blinking buttons, metallic panels, and strangers around him. The window directly in front of him shimmered with bright lights. Millions of stars in a dark sky.

"We're in outer space!" he yelled. They were on a ship. A real spaceship.

"Sir?" the man beside him asked. "Of course we are in space. Are you well, Captain Sanchez?"

Luis frowned. He looked at Tyler and Casey. Why was the man calling him captain? Couldn't he see that it was three kids sitting at the controls?

Tyler reached out and tapped the man in the knee with one of his crutches.

The man glanced at him. "Yes?"

Tyler raised his eyebrows. "Uh, do you know me?" he asked.

"Know you, sir? Of course, Mr. Jenson. You are first officer."

Tyler grinned. "Cool."

The man in green pointed at the large view port in front of them. "We have five minutes to impact, Captain. If we don't slow the ship, we will crash into the space station."

Luis's mouth fell open. He looked around the room. Men and women were watching him, clearly expecting him to lead. He turned to the window and watched the large,

TAP!

TAP!

long object floating in space. It was getting larger as they sped toward it.

The space station was all blinking lights and smooth edges. It was mostly white, with different sections of brightly colored steel. It looked like a floating mall.

Luis's voice shook. "But . . . but . . . why don't you just slow down the ship?"

A tall man in a gray uniform walked over to stand in front of Luis. "We cannot change our speed without your order, sir."

Luis looked at Tyler. He didn't look afraid. He was grinning. They were in space. It was Tyler's dream come true.

"Uh, well, slow the ship then," Luis said, his voice coming out in a croak.

The man nodded. "Captain's orders! Bring her into the docking port at half speed."

A green-haired woman said, "Bringing her in, sir." She pressed buttons, then waved her hand across a screen that floated in the air. The space station seemed to stop, but Luis realized it was because their ship was slowing.

Luis held his breath. Why were they listening to him? Three strange kids show up on a spaceship and everyone thinks they're officers? They didn't even seem surprised.

Where were they? Or more importantly, *when* were they? He remembered how the dates sped by in the time machine. How far into the future had they gone?

A huge panel in the space station opened. He imagined guards rushing to arrest him and his friends as they docked.

He leaned over and whispered to Casey, "What happened? Where's the time machine?"

Casey shrugged. She didn't look as scared as Luis felt, or as excited as Tyler looked. Luis knew she was thinking and studying. This was something completely new to learn.

"Red alert!" someone screamed.

Sirens blared and the ship shook. Luis fell sideways in his chair as the ship tilted.

"Are we crashing?" he yelled.

People were shouting as they pressed more buttons and spoke into intercoms.

"We are turning away from the space station," the man in gray said. "We are passing the docking bay."

"At least we aren't crashing," Luis whispered.

The man walked around Luis and pointed at the starry window. "But we are veering away from our course."

Before Luis could ask what that meant, the ship picked up speed. It shot past the edge of the space station. Luis stared at empty space. No space station, no planets, nothing but darkness and stars.

"Can we turn the ship around and go back?" Casey asked.

Tyler jumped out of his seat. "Yeah, just turn us around. Make a U-turn. Do a spin."

One of the crew stepped out from a nearby screen. "First Officer Jenson, as a scientist, you should know the answer to that question."

Tyler grinned. "Oh yes, that's me. First Officer Tyler. Of course I know."

Luis raised his eyebrows and Tyler shrugged.

A voice came from all around them. Luis whirled in his chair, then realized it was coming from an intercom above him.

"Captain, this is Chief Engineer Peterson. Something is jamming the engines. They won't slow. They won't stop. I can't steer the ship."

Luis swallowed hard. "Does that mean we just keep going farther into space?"

The man in gray nodded. "Yes. Unless we regain control of the ship, we will just keep moving farther away from the space station and from Earth."

"So what," Tyler said. "We're a spaceship. We can just go back, right?"

"There is more, Captain," Engineer Peterson's voice said. "Please, come to the engine room."

Luis cleared his throat. He stood. His dream was coming true. A real adventure just like in the books he loved. "I'm needed in the engine room."

"Up," Casey whispered.

The man in gray frowned. "Down, Lieutenant Jenson."

Casey said, "Oops, I forgot."

There were whispers and everyone stared. A man stepped forward. "Excuse me, ma'am, would you like me to escort you to sick bay?"

Casey frowned. Before she could say anything, Luis grabbed her arm. He nodded to Tyler.

"Thank you, she'll be fine. She's just had a shock," Luis said. "We . . . the three of us are going to the engine room."

Everyone stood as they left the room.

Luis glanced at the men and women moving around them. No one seemed surprised to see three kids without uniforms wandering down the long hallway. Instead, they saluted Luis and hurried past as sirens blared.

"What's going on? Why do they think you're the captain and I'm a lieutenant?" Casey asked.

Luis shook his head. He looked around, wondering which way the nearest elevator was and whether he would even recognize one.

"I don't know. That machine isn't just a regular time machine like I've read about in books. Maybe it changed us. These people think we're supposed to be here. They aren't even shocked that we're kids," Luis said.

Casey reached over and pinched Tyler. He yelped. She said, "We're not holograms. It's like we're here, but they can't see who we really are. Or they don't care."

Luis stepped in front of a man walking past them and cleared his throat. "Can you tell us where the elevator is? We need to go to the engine room."

The man, in a tan jumpsuit, took a step back. "Yes, Captain, the nearest elevator is where it's always been." He pointed. "Around that corner."

"Oh, yes, I remember," Luis said, making his voice sound gruff.

"Let's go, Lieutenant Jenson, Mr. Jenson, and, um . . ." he said to Casey and Tyler.

The crewman frowned and hurried away.

They turned the corner. Luis nodded each time someone saluted him. It would be fun being the captain of a spaceship. He'd seen enough movies to know that the hero was sometimes brave, sometimes scared, but always did his best.

"There," Tyler said, tugging at Luis's sleeve.

Doors in the hall opened and people in different-colored uniforms stepped off the elevator. They stopped talking when they saw Luis and his friends.

Luis ran inside the elevator, his heart pounding. Tyler and Casey followed, and the door closed behind them.

"Where are the buttons?" Casey asked.

"I bet we don't need any." Luis cleared his throat. "Elevator, take us to the engine room."

"Yes, Captain," a voice said.

"Cool!" Casey said.

The elevator moved in silence. A white light above them moved back and forth, then turned green. The door opened.

Luis walked out of the elevator into a large room full of people and machines. Both were making lots of noise.

"Captain!" someone yelled.

A woman in a black uniform hurried toward them from across the room. Luis glanced at her name tag. Chief Engineer Peterson.

"Uh, hello," Luis said.

She frowned. "Sir, I needed to speak to you alone."

Luis looked at his friends. "But I need them. It's okay for them to listen."

Peterson nodded. "We have a major problem. Ensign Carter said that moments after we were given the order to move toward the space station, he received a message from you to override the original course and speed up. Now, we've lost complete control of the ship."

Luis's eyes went wide. "But, I didn't call anyone."

Engineer Peterson frowned at him. "Then someone has impersonated you, Captain Sanchez. And put us on a dangerous course."

Casey put her hands on her hips. "Can't you just change everything back from down here?"

"We've tried, but someone has jammed our computers. They don't recognize anyone who had clearance. They don't respond to our input at all," the engineer said. "Try it yourself."

Luis followed her to a console. She pressed a button and nodded at him.

Luis bent down and cleared his throat. "Computer, I need you to slow the ship and turn it back to the space station. Okay?"

The computer was silent a moment. Then a voice said, "This voice is not recognized for such a command. All such codes have been changed."

Luis growled at the computer. What did he know about spaceships and computers in the future?

Here was a great adventure. Hadn't he wanted this? A real one, not just reading about them?

"How much time before we are too far to turn back?" Luis asked.

Engineer Peterson pulled something from her pocket that looked like a calculator. She spoke into it and then squinted at its small screen.

"If we do not regain control of the ship, we will stay on a course that will take us into enemy territory. If we do regain control of the ship, we still have a problem. The engines are working hard at this increased speed. Too hard. They'll blow if we can't slow down." She put a hand on Luis's shoulder. "You have to find the one who has taken over the engine room and gain control again."

The engineer walked away as someone shouted her name.

Tyler said, "You wanted adventure, Luis. I wanted to go into space. And Casey wanted to learn something new."

Luis folded his arms. "Yeah, and it looks like we're responsible for this ship and its crew. We need to figure out what to do."

As the ship trembled, Luis took a deep breath. He was captain of a runaway ship. It was time to face real adventure.

MEETING UNCLE CYRUS

The ship shuddered, and Luis fought to keep from falling.

"The ship's speed has increased. She won't take much more," a man shouted.

At least, Luis thought he was a man. He towered at least seven feet tall. His long orange beard lay flat against his chest like a hairy necklace.

Tyler leaned against a tall machine and stared up at the bearded man. He gave the man a squint-eyed look. "How can a ship go too fast? I mean, this is the future. It's a spaceship, not a hot air balloon."

The bearded man bent down to look into Tyler's face. "There is no future for this old ship. The USS *Phoenix* could break apart with this kind of speed. Come with me. I'll show you the already damaged power crystals."

Tyler walked over to a group of workers and talked loudly about the ship's engines. He moved quickly, his crutches shining red from the flashing lights around him.

Luis watched his best friend. They were on a spaceship, something Tyler had always dreamed of doing. Did the time machine know about their dreams?

Casey grabbed Luis's arm. "We have to do something. If you are the captain, you must have some of his memories."

Luis shook his head. He whispered, "No, I don't. None of us exactly know what we're doing. We're just going to have to figure it out."

He walked across the room and out the door.

Luis waited in the corridor for Casey and Tyler. Tyler grinned at them. "Maybe we aren't really here. Maybe we aren't really in danger. This could just be an amazing dream. It's so exciting!"

Casey pinched him again. "We're really here."

Tyler said, "That's even more exciting. I could learn a lot. When we get home, I could apply for NASA and be the youngest astronaut ever."

His sister nodded. "But we're on a doomed ship, Tyler. It's not a museum or space school."

Luis said, "We need to find a place to talk where no one can hear us."

"What about the captain's quarters?" Casey said.

"Good idea," Luis said. They walked back to the elevator.

Tyler spoke first. "Captain's quarters!"

"Yes, sir," the elevator voice said.

They moved back up through the ship. The door opened into a large room with dark wood furniture. Shelves were filled with books about space, small models of sailing ships, and framed pictures of a man in uniform.

Luis picked up one of the pictures.

"This must be the real captain. So why do people think I'm the captain now?" he asked.

Casey stared into a large silver mirror. "Are we holograms or is this some story we've jumped into and not really somewhere in time?"

Luis said, "Since we can feel things, I think we're really here. For some reason, the crew sees us as if we're supposed to be here. Maybe when the machine sends us somewhere, we suddenly belong."

"Wow," Tyler said. He hurried to a lighted desk with a 3-D map of the galaxy. When he reached for Saturn's rings, the map began to move. The planets rotated around the sun.

"Amazing," Casey said.

Luis sat in a large, cushioned chair behind the desk. "Yeah, loads of fun. No time for playing. We're in big trouble. We've got to figure out how to get home. How do we find the time machine? Where did it go?"

"It didn't go anywhere. The machine is where you left it. You are the ones who traveled in time," a voice said.

Luis gasped and pointed across the room.

A wispy man stood beside a brass telescope. He flickered in and out, like a ghost or a television program with bad reception.

"Who are you?" Luis shouted.

The man bowed. "I am Cyrus Sanchez."

Luis backed away. "Uncle Cyrus? But, you're dead. My dad just inherited your estate!"

The ghostly man shook his head. His head moved in slow motion. "Time means nothing to me any longer. I'm not dead. I am stuck in the machine. But I am pleased to meet a great-great-great-great-nephew."

"You're stuck in the machine?" Luis asked.

The shadowy figure moved to look out a small window. "Not exactly in the machine, but in the expanse of time created by the machine. And I am sorry to bear bad news, but if you do not solve the mystery on this ship, you will also be stuck in the machine's pull, forever moving through time," Uncle Cyrus said. "You are in greater danger than what is happening on this ship. Sending humans through the machine seems to have altered it somehow."

Luis walked around the desk. He stood in front of the flickering man.

"Can't you help us?" Luis asked. "You invented the machine. Can't you fix it?"

Uncle Cyrus shook his head again. The layered movements made Luis's eyes cross.

"Tesla was a genius. I'm sure he tried to rescue me, but he's gone now. I am trapped. It seems that I can appear wherever the time machine sends people. No one has used it since I set those dials many, many years ago." He frowned and sighed. "I wish you had not used it."

Luis swallowed hard. "Maybe we shouldn't have, but we're here now. Maybe you are here to help us find whoever caused all this trouble and save these people."

Uncle Cyrus turned to the porthole. He stared into space. "You must solve this problem yourselves. But I can tell you that if you find that strange metallic cat that came with you, you will be closer to discovering the enemy on this ship. I am sorry, but I am having trouble maintaining this form."

And like a balloon, Uncle Cyrus disappeared with a pop and a whoosh of air.

"Okay, that was weird," Casey said. She picked up a small model ship and began pulling it apart.

Luis watched her for a moment. He knew working helped her think. "I don't want to be stuck in time with Uncle Cyrus."

The ship lurched again. Tyler fell into a chair. Casey dropped parts of the model.

Luis grabbed the corner of the desk. "I think this ship is moving even faster. We'd better find Tyler's cat."

Tyler moved toward the door. "I told you Steel was a great invention. It will come when I call if I'm within thirty feet of its sensors."

The hallways were full of people running and yelling orders. Tyler pushed his way against the stream of people. Luis knew that deep down, Tyler was loving every minute of this space adventure.

Whenever someone passed them, they nodded and said, "Captain!" Luis nodded back. He imagined reading about himself, the hero of a spaceship lost somewhere in space and time.

"Anything from Steel yet?" Luis asked.

Tyler shouted back, "Nothing! Let's get away from this crowd."

They turned down a side corridor.

"Steel!" Casey called.

"It only responds to my voice," Tyler said. "Steel!"

"That figures," Casey said.

The hallway seemed to narrow and soon there were no doors.

"I think we need to go back," Luis said.

"Quiet!" Tyler ordered. "I hear something."

They stopped.

"I don't hear anything," Casey said. "That weird cat isn't around here. And now we're lost."

MEOWEEE! BOING!

Tyler pointed to the end of the hall. "Steel! Come here. Now!"

When they reached the corridor's end, they could still hear the cat's weird yowls.

"Where is it? Behind the wall?" Luis asked.

Casey said, "Leave it to that stupid cat to not be any help at all." She folded her arms and leaned against the wall.

The wall glowed blue and they heard a loud click. Luis pulled Casey away.

A door appeared. A red button in the middle of it glowed on and off.

"Cool!" Tyler said. He pressed the button.

Nothing happened. Tyler pushed and pushed. "Stupid invisible door!"

"Wait, let me try," Luis said. He put his finger against the red button. It glowed even brighter. Then the door popped open.

"I guess only the captain can open it," Luis said.

They stared into the blackness.

"Steel?" Tyler whispered.

From the darkness, there was the sound of metal and something flew out the door.

MEORRR! BOING!

Steel turned its head toward Tyler. Its eyes were red and its tail spun in circles.

Then Steel did something the robot cat had never done. It spoke one word, "Danger!" Then it disappeared down the corridor.

Inside the room, something moved in the darkness. Something big.

CHAPTER FIVE

A Big, Scary Robot

The sound of the robot cat's weird meowing echoed down the hall. Luis backed away from the dark room. He reached his hand toward the open door, but the flashing button he had touched was gone.

Tyler leaned against his crutches. "Wow, did you hear that? Steel spoke. A real word."

Casey pointed down the corridor. "Yeah, but did you hear what that word was?"

Luis nodded. "Danger. And if a robot cat could look afraid, Steel looked terrified."

From inside the dark room, they heard clanks and crashes.

"Something else is in that room," Casey said. "And it's big."

They stared at the open door. From somewhere down the corridor, they could hear Steel's voice shouting, "Danger! Danger!"

"Um, I think we'd better follow Steel," Tyler said. "Someone has been messing with it. My robot's never said anything other than that messed up meowing before."

A loud hiss came from the dark room. Luis backed away, pulling his friends with him. Something filled the doorway. Luis blinked.

It was a robot. But not like Steel. It was a shiny, red, manlike robot, and it was as tall and wide as the doorway. It stared at them with bulging eyes that glowed from a square head as big as a microwave.

Casey gasped. "Now *that's* a robot."

"A big, scary robot," Luis said. "I don't think he'll let you take him apart to see how he works."

The robot stepped out of the room. His metal feet hit the floor with a clang. One hand was like a human's, the other like a lobster's claw. The claw reached toward them.

"Run!" Tyler shouted. He rushed past Luis, his crutches sliding across the floor.

Luis pushed Casey in front of him. They ran down the hall, yelling at Tyler, who had disappeared down another corridor.

"Is that thing following us?" Casey asked.

Luis glanced back. The robot still stood in the doorway. Luis hoped he couldn't move down the narrow corridor. But with a sudden turn, he crashed toward them, smashing his fist against the wall as he moved.

"Faster!" Luis ordered.

Casey turned the direction her brother had gone. "Tyler!"

"This way!" Tyler called.

Luis and Casey followed the voice until they saw Tyler's foot and a crutch sticking out of a doorway.

"Hurry, you two," Tyler said. "This door is made of steel. We should be safe in here."

Casey ran inside. Luis bent over to catch his breath. He looked behind him and saw the robot turn down the corridor.

Luis yelped when Casey grabbed his shirt and yanked him into the room. She slammed a button and the door closed behind him.

"Where are we?" Luis asked.

The room was big and dark, but Luis could see shapes. He hoped there wasn't something else dangerous inside with them.

The door rattled as the robot passed by. Luis held his breath, afraid to make a sound. Outside, everything was quiet.

"Don't say a word," Casey whispered.

Then they heard a noise, as if someone was sniffing very loudly.

"Is he smelling us?" Tyler asked.

"Eeewww," Casey said. "That's just nasty."

"Quiet," Luis said.

There was more silence. Then the room seemed to explode with loud banging. The steel door rattled and shook. A large dent appeared in it, then another.

"He's going to get inside!" Casey screamed.

Luis felt along the wall until he came to a button. He pressed it over and over. Finally, he waved his hand over it. Lights flooded the room.

"Why can't the future make up its mind? Buttons or scanners," Luis said.

The room was lined with shiny, clean metal sinks. Long metal tables and chairs filled the floor. Huge pots and pans hung from the ceiling.

"We're in the galley," Luis said.

"The what?" Casey asked.

"The kitchen!" Tyler exclaimed.

"Well, perfect," Luis said. "A good place for a giant red monster robot to mash us up and cook us."

Luis looked around the room for another exit. He didn't see anything.

"There's only one door in and out," Luis said. "And that robot is on the other side of it."

They ran around the room, looking for something to use to fight the robot.

Casey picked up a large pot. "This wouldn't even tickle that big metal creature."

Finally, the robot burst through the door.

They turned as the robot stepped into the galley. His huge head moved until it looked right at Luis. The robot's claw hand began to spin.

"Uh-oh," Luis said. "You two run around behind it," he yelled. "He doesn't want you. Find help."

Tyler shook his head. He raised one of his crutches at the robot stalking toward them. "No way are we leaving you. Right, Casey?"

Casey didn't answer. Luis wondered if she had already run out the door.

"Hurry, I found something," Casey yelled.

Luis and Tyler turned and saw Casey crawling into a small hole in the wall.

"A dumbwaiter to send the food to other decks," she said. "I'm going down. I'll send it right back and you follow me."

A panel slid shut and she was gone. A moment later, the panel opened and the hole was empty.

"Go!" Luis shouted.

Tyler hurried to the hole. He pushed himself inside. One of his crutches fell onto the floor.

Luis grabbed it, then whispered, "Go now."

Tyler disappeared behind the sliding panel.

Luis looked up. The robot was in front of him. Luis swung at him with Tyler's crutch.

The robot grabbed the crutch in his claw and pulled. Luis held onto it with both hands.

"Let go, you metal monster! That belongs to my best friend and you can't have it!" Luis yanked as hard as he could.

The robot held tight. Luis saw a heavy ladle on the floor. He held onto the crutch with one hand and leaned forward. His fingers brushed against the end of the ladle.

With a grunt, he reached farther. His other arm ached as he kept hold of the crutch.

"There!" he shouted as he grabbed the curved edge of the ladle handle. He swung it as hard as he could toward the robot's head and let it go. It flew into the air, smacking against the robot's glowing red eyes.

The eyes turned black. The robot bent forward. His claw opened and the crutch fell.

Luis cheered, "All right! Look who beat the giant robot! Me, Luis Sanchez, that's who!"

With a whir of gears from inside, the robot's eyes turned red again. He moved.

Luis scrambled off the floor and dove into the dumbwaiter. He held tight to Tyler's crutch as the robot's metal hand moved toward him.

Then the panel in front of him closed with a whoosh and he was falling. Fast. Through the darkness.

He had only a moment to yell when he stopped moving and the panel opened.

Luis rolled out of the hole and looked for his friends.

Casey and Tyler were waiting.

Their hands were tied. They looked at him with wide eyes.

Behind them, three men were also waiting. Men with lasers. Men with reptile skin and long mouths. Mouths full of sharp teeth.

They pointed their lasers at him. Luis stood and raised his arms.

CAPTAIN ZARLOK

"Hey, what's going on here?" Luis asked.

Casey shouted, "We've been captured. Run!"

Luis backed away. One of the lizard creatures stepped forward, pointing his laser weapon.

"This is like a bad science fiction movie. A low-budget Star Trek," Tyler said. "*Robot Man and Lizard Aliens.*"

The tallest lizard creature said, "I am Captain Zarlok of the planet Nim. We have your crew. You cannot escape."

Luis folded his arms and tried to sound like a grown-up. "So, what do you want? We've got enough problems on this ship. Someone has taken over our computers and sent us speeding through space. There's a giant robot chasing us."

Captain Zarlok smiled. It wasn't a friendly smile. "Yes, we know. We have set your ship on a different course. And the robot is ours."

"Why?" Luis asked.

"How?" Casey asked.

Captain Zarlok began to shimmer and change. Suddenly, he looked like a human.

"We have learned your computer languages. You are hearing my language as your own. I simply made a call to your engineer in your voice, then reset your computers to accept only my voice," he said through a human mouth.

"Wait, you look familiar," Luis said.

Tyler struggled in the bindings around his wrists. "Of course he does. He looks like you. I mean, the captain you, with the uniform."

Captain Zarlok nodded. "We can shift our appearance. Now that I have you, I can go to the bridge and no one will know that I am not you. Before long, my whole crew will be aboard."

Luis now knew what the danger was that Steel had warned them about. But how could he and his friends, plus one cowardly robot cat and the fading shadow of his four-greats uncle stop an army of lizard men?

"Why are you here?" he asked.

"Our ship's power is dying. Your ship's technology is adequate. We need it to get us to your Earth and other planets that we will conquer," Zarlok said.

The other two lizard men shimmered and shook until they looked like a man and a woman.

"Now we are like you three. No one will know the difference," Captain Zarlok said.

"I think he means they look like Tyler and me," Casey said. "I mean, the ones we look like to everyone here."

The lizard man cocked his head, his still-large eyes blinking. "I do not know what this means, female, but we are in charge now."

He nodded to the other aliens. They pushed Luis and his friends across the room and into a storage closet. They closed the door.

"There's no lock on this door," Casey whispered. "Unless they leave a guard, we can get out easily."

"Too late," Luis said, peering through a small window in the door. "Here comes our old friend."

He watched the giant robot thunder into the room. Captain Zarlok spoke to him. The robot marched across the room and stood in front of the storage door.

"We're stuck in here now," Luis said.

He slid down to the floor. He felt bad for the ship's crew. Now there was *another* fake captain. He felt worse for him and his friends. They were doomed to be stuck in time like Uncle Cyrus.

Luis kicked his foot against the wall. This was his first real adventure. He wasn't going to let a bunch of big lizards ruin it.

"We've got to get out of here and warn the rest of the crew," Casey whispered.

Tyler pointed at the door. "How? There's a giant robot guarding the door and no other way out of here."

"Then we have to get rid of that robot," Casey said.

She reached into one of her jacket pockets and pulled out a small red object.

"I don't think a cell phone is going to work in space and in the future," Luis said.

Casey grinned at him. "Maybe not, but this isn't a phone. It's a small two-way radio I brought. I thought we might use it while we checked out the shed. Someone could've been a lookout in case our dads came back."

"So," Tyler said, "how will that help us?"

"The other one is attached to your cat. I attached it when Steel first rolled by us."

Luis said, "You're a genius, Casey!"

Casey pressed a button and a green light flickered on. She held out the radio to Tyler. "Now you don't have to be less than 30 feet away. Call your silly cat."

Tyler pressed the box against his mouth. "Steel, I need you to come now. I need you to follow this signal."

The radio crackled. Tyler pressed the button again and repeated his command.

"How will we know if Steel hears it?" Luis asked.

"When it shows up," Tyler said.

Luis pounded on the closet door. The robot bent down and put his face against the little window. Luis stuck out his tongue. The eyes blinked red. Luis turned away and leaned against the door. "Do you think the aliens have taken over the ship already?"

Casey shrugged. "Maybe. Maybe not. But we've got to get out of here, stop the aliens, and fix the ship before it blows up. Then we just have to get back home."

Tyler dropped the radio in his lap. "Oh, is that all?"

MEOWWRRR! BOING!

Tyler grabbed the radio. "Hey, did you hear that? Steel must've heard me!"

Casey said, "Great. Tell that cat to get its metal tail over here."

Tyler whispered into the box. A moment later, they heard a clang as the robot turned away from the door and stomped his foot hard on the floor.

"Uh-oh," Luis said.

"Steel! Are you okay?" Tyler shouted.

Silence.

Tyler banged a crutch against the door. "You better not hurt him you overgrown tin can!"

Luis peered through the window. At first, he saw only the galley full of pots and pans.

Then he saw a shadow. A large shadow. The robot stomped across the room, roaring like an angry metal supervillain. Luis watched as something streaked between the robot's feet. The robot turned. Steel went in circles around the robot. The robot roared again and spun in a circle. His claw hand reached for the cat.

But Steel moved faster and kept away from it. Steel's metal tail moved up and down as if to give it speed.

The robot wobbled. He spun again and again. Steel moved between the robot's feet once more. The red giant raised its foot above Steel.

The robot man lost his balance and toppled sideways, crashing into the metal tables. Steel neared the robot's body and stared into his eyes. Laser beams streamed from Steel's eyes. The robot's eyes turned black and his arms fell limp.

Luis waited, but this time the robot didn't move again.

"Wow," Tyler said. "Steel completely knocked out his sensors."

Luis and Casey high-fived, and then Casey hugged her brother. "I guess that metal meower isn't so dumb after all."

With a click, the closet door opened. Steel stood by the door, its head cocked.

"Move quickly. Those aliens are not wasting time."

Tyler bent down to touch the robot cat. "You talked again! Whole sentences!"

"I may be old, but I can still make sense," the cat said.

Luis grabbed Steel and held him close to his face. The cat seemed to shimmer. A shadow surrounded him.

"Uncle Cyrus? Is that you?" Luis asked.

From Steel's voice box, Uncle Cyrus sounded like a crackling transmission from an old radio. "It is I. Trapped for decades, I have but watched and learned. It is difficult for me to show myself, but I have reprogrammed this robot so you can hear my voice. Put the cat down and let us save this ship and get you all home."

Luis put Steel on the floor. He and his friends followed the cat into the corridor to battle the lizard men.

CHAPTER SEVEN

Run!

Luis fell against a wall as the ship rocked again. Why didn't the lizard men stop this? Soon there would be no ship left worth stealing!

They walked through the quiet corridor until they reached the elevator. Luis didn't see anyone else. He didn't like the quietness. Where were all the people who had been rushing around in a panic before? Could the lizard aliens have captured everyone on the ship?

Luis followed the robot cat that was now a two-way radio with his uncle Cyrus who should have died long, long ago. This whole adventure was getting weirder and weirder.

"Bridge," Uncle Cyrus said. Steel sat in the middle of the elevator.

Luis watched the elevator door. What would be happening on the bridge when the door opened? If the aliens looked like people, how could they tell anyone apart?

The elevator stopped. "Here we go!" Luis shouted.

Casey stepped out as the door slid open.

It was chaos! People and lizard men filled the bridge, battling one another. A control panel sparked as a lizard man swung around, smashing his tail on the console.

Luis saw the man in silver who had stood beside Luis's chair when they first arrived. He grabbed a lizard man and pinned his arms behind him. But the creature burst free, pushed the man into a chair, and put his booted foot against the man's chest.

The man looked at the elevator. His mouth dropped and he jerked his head and mouthed, "Captain! Go!"

Luis stood still, terrified to leave or stay. He yelled as a man in a red uniform was shoved into the elevator. The man slid to the floor and groaned.

"Don't worry, I'll save the ship!" Luis shouted to the crew. Somehow, he believed he really would.

A lizard man came toward them, hissing.

"Get back, Casey!" Tyler yelled.

Luis pulled her back into the elevator and said, "Engine room!"

The lizard man pushed his tail into the closing door. Tyler took one of his crutches and beat it against the tail until the lizard hissed louder and pulled away. The door closed and the elevator began to move.

The man on the floor blinked several times. He moaned, then looked at Steel and yelped. He turned away and gasped when he saw Luis and his friends.

With a grunt, he rolled to his knees and tried to stand. "Ensign Carver, Captain, sir, the ship is being overtaken."

Luis nodded. "Yes, we know. Do you know how many of those lizard things there are on the bridge?"

Ensign Carver put his hand against his forehead as if to press the information into his head. "The three of you burst onto the bridge and ordered us to stay where we were. Then, you . . . they . . . changed into lizards. All of a sudden, several of the crew seemed to turn fuzzy and became more of the lizard things." Ensign Carver continued. "Perhaps a dozen. Maybe more. The elevator arrived, filled with them before you came back."

Then he closed his eyes and fell forward.

Casey bent down beside the ensign. "Dad made us take a first-aid course last summer." She put her fingers to the man's neck and pulled back an eyelid. "I think he's just unconscious. Probably shock."

With a shudder, the elevator stopped. The lights flickered.

"This isn't the engine room's floor," Luis said. "Open elevator door!"

The elevator voice was silent.

Steel stood up on his hind legs, leaning on his tail.

"Perhaps you should ask this metal cat to try," Uncle Cyrus's voice said. "It might be able to communicate with other electrical things. It's worth a try, anyway."

Tyler bent down to his cat. He spoke slowly into its ear. "We need this elevator door to open."

Steel beeped and squawked. The elevator voice beeped and squawked back. After a moment, the door slid open.

"Where are we?" Casey asked. She picked up Steel. "Uncle Cyrus, do you have a plan? And if you couldn't solve your own time travel problem, are you sure you can solve ours?"

Uncle Cyrus said, "As I told you, I cannot solve the problem. I can only give advice. This is the first time someone has used Tesla's machine since I became trapped. I do not know how long I will be with you."

"Then we better figure this out soon," Luis said. "We must be here for a reason. Maybe without us, the crew and this ship would become evil-alien prisoners."

They stepped carefully out of the elevator. They were the only ones in the corridor. Luis put a finger to his lips. He and Casey grabbed the unconscious man by the arms and dragged him out of the elevator. The crewman mumbled and groaned and then his eyes flew open.

Ensign Carver jumped up, wobbled a little, and tried to stand straight as he saluted Luis. "I apologize, sir, I may have blacked out for a moment."

Luis said, "Quiet, Ensign Carver. We don't know if any of those lizard men are around."

"Where are we?" Casey asked again.

Tyler walked over to a small screen near the elevator. He poked at one of the buttons. He looked more closely at the screen. "Looks like we're back where we escaped from that robot. The galley is right there."

"Uh-oh," Casey said. "We don't want to find that robot moving around again."

Luis looked down at Steel. "Uncle Cyrus, can this cat talk to the robot like it did to the elevator?"

"Yes, I believe it can do that," Uncle Cyrus replied.

Tyler said, "Are you sure that's a good idea? If Steel wakes the robot and can't communicate, he'll just stomp my cat into the ground."

Luis closed his eyes. He thought about all the adventure books he'd read and movies he'd watched. There had to be a way to win against the lizard aliens.

Maybe, with the combination of the cat's computerized talents and Uncle Cyrus's scientific brain, and the combined smartness of his friends, maybe they had a chance.

He snapped his fingers. "I have an idea."

"Let's hear it," Casey said.

Luis had an idea. But it might be a terrible one. A ridiculous one. A dangerous one.

He took a deep breath. "If Steel can talk to the robot, we're going to make sure that he will only listen to me and not Captain Zarlok."

"How?" Tyler asked.

"You're going to reprogram him, that's how. You created that cat. You've broken into school computers to change the bell schedule. You're smart about this stuff," Luis said.

Luis looked at his friends. "And then, we're going to use the robot to help us capture Captain Zarlok and the rest of the lizard aliens."

A BIG, HELPFUL ROBOT

Before his friends could stop staring bug-eyed at him and give him any more arguments, Luis grabbed Steel and hurried down the hall. He glanced back at the injured man.

"Ensign, get to sick bay and find the medical officer. Tell anyone you see what's going on. Lock yourselves in."

Luis hurried to the galley. The door was open. He peeked inside.

He yelped as something grabbed his shoulder.

"It's just us," Casey whispered. "Do you see the robot? Or any lizard men?"

Luis shook his head. "Not so far." He put Steel on the floor. "Okay, cat, see if that creepy robot is still knocked out."

Steel rolled into the room. Luis flinched at the sound of the rollers on the floor. Couldn't Tyler have made it as quiet as a real cat?

Luis, Casey, and Tyler waited.

"Maybe we should just go inside," Casey said. "That cat is probably bits and pieces of robot parts by now."

She yelped when Steel rolled out of the room and stopped at Luis's feet. Uncle Cyrus said, "It appears that the robot is still shut down. Are you going to tell this cat to turn him on again?"

"Can't you?" Luis asked.

"No. At least not yet," Cyrus said. "I am not *in* the cat. My voice comes through its speakers, but I am still trapped in time."

Tyler grabbed Luis's arm. "We need to reprogram him *before* we wake him up."

Luis nodded, and they slipped into the room. The robot lay where he had fallen. Tyler sat down beside him.

Tyler ran his hands around the robot's chest and head. "There must be a way inside. He has to have a control panel or something." Tyler's hands stopped moving. He bent forward and said, "There is something on his neck."

Tyler's fingers pulled at the edges of a raised square section. "This must be the way in. But how am I going to get the panel off?"

Casey reached into the largest pocket of her jacket. She pulled out a small purple toolbox. "Good thing I don't go anywhere without this."

Casey opened the box and rummaged through it. She looked at the panel, back at the box, then back at the panel. "Nope. Not this one. Maybe. Nope. Ah, here it is."

Casey pulled out a screwdriver with an odd-shaped end. "Of course, this is alien technology, but I can make anything work. Usually."

She pushed and twisted and turned the tool against the bolts on the panel. Luis held his breath. If she couldn't get the computer compartment open so Tyler could reprogram this monster, Luis would have to come up with plan B. The problem was, he only had plan A. And even that one wasn't perfect.

"Hurry," Tyler said. "Those lizard guys could show up any minute."

With a final twist, Casey shouted, "Eureka!" She tugged at the panel and it slid open.

Tyler said, "Okay, Sis, move! My turn."

He leaned over the opening. Lights were blinking on a panel inside. "Wow, this is pretty amazing. I sure hope I can figure it out."

Luis hadn't thought about that. This wasn't a robot at the college lab where Tyler liked to hang out. It wasn't a science kit he put together. It was alien and it was from the future. Tyler was the smartest guy Luis knew when it came to computers and robots, but this was different from anything they'd ever seen before.

"If the lizard aliens find out what we're doing before Tyler finishes, what will we do next?" Casey asked as Tyler worked.

Luis didn't want to think about it, so he sat down by Steel. "Uncle Cyrus, what happened to you that got you stuck in time?" he asked.

Cyrus's voice let out a sigh through Steel's speakers. "Tesla didn't want me to go, but I just had to try it. Someone needed to. It had to be one of us. And if Tesla didn't return, the world would have lost someone very important."

"I bet you were important too," Luis said.

"To some, but it wasn't the same," Cyrus said. "I didn't tell Tesla that I was going. I snuck in one night and set the dials for 1921, twenty-five years in the future. I had always dreamed of the future. And it was fantastic. Airplanes! New automobiles! The assembly line!"

"Work, you piece of alien junk!" Tyler growled, banging on the control panel.

"Don't break it!" Casey shouted.

"Quiet!" Tyler shouted back.

"But, what happened that made you not be able to go back to your time" Luis asked, putting Steel on his lap. "And where have you been all this . . . time?"

Cyrus said, "I don't know what there is in that machine that throws you directly toward a problem. I was involved in the detection of a great mystery with the police. I was surprised when they assumed I was one of them. I was to help the chief inspector. But when threatened by a gangster, I became afraid and fled with information that would have solved the case. After that, the inspector disappeared and I could not get home.

"But as to where I have been, I do not know. I am as a ghost in time. I could speak to no one and but watch the world around me. It was as if I were invisible to all until you turned the machine on again. I never saw my wife or son again. He was only a baby."

Luis hung his head. He should never have let his friends talk him into going into the shed, let alone getting into the time machine.

Noise filled the room. Luis gasped as the robot stood to his full height. His red eyes stared at Luis. His clawed hand opened and closed.

"Everyone run!" Luis said. He crab-crawled backward away from the robot.

Tyler stuck one of his crutches behind Luis and said, "Wait."

Tyler spoke clearly into Steel's ear. "Okay, tell him who's in charge now."

Steel rolled forward and stopped to stare up at the robot. The cat sent out a series of beeps and clicks.

The giant robot's eyes blinked on and off. He bent toward Luis. He turned his head as if listening. And he did not attack.

Luis jumped up and slapped Tyler on his back. "You did it!"

"Excuse me," Casey said. "*We* did it." She closed up her little box of tools and stuffed them into her jacket pocket.

Luis socked the robot in the arm. He yelped as his hand smashed into metal. "Okay, new friend. Here are your orders. Find the lizard men and capture them. I want them kept under control until this ship reaches the space station again. All of them."

The robot straightened. He turned toward the door and stomped out of the room.

"And no smashing!" Luis called after him. "Just capture them."

He had a feeling the real captain would want to talk with these aliens. And, he needed to get Zarlok to change the control of the ship.

Luis, Casey, Tyler, and Steel followed behind the robot. He headed out the door and down the hall. Soon they heard the whoosh of the elevator door. They hoped it was working okay.

"I sure hope he fits inside," Tyler said.

The robot bent down and walked into the elevator. Steel slipped in between his feet.

Tyler stepped inside, sliding beside the robot.

"I'm not getting on with that thing. It's like having 100 people in one elevator," Casey said.

"This is a spaceship," Tyler said. "We're not at the mall. The elevator can hold us."

Casey sighed and stepped inside.

Luis took a deep breath and ordered, "Bridge."

The elevator moved upward. Luis said, "I am the captain. I can do this." Before he could think about what was about to happen, the door slid open.

The bridge looked like a room full of twins. Men and women in different-colored uniforms sat on the floor, their arms crossed behind their heads. Next to some of them stood an identical twin. Other people sat in front of control panels. Their bodies shifted from human to lizard form.

"Stop the lizard people!" Luis shouted.

The robot stepped forward. His eyes glowed bright red.

"Capture the aliens!" Luis called.

Captain Zarlok snarled at the robot. "Stop! I order you!"

The robot stopped and looked at the leader of the lizard people. His head swiveled and he looked back at Luis.

Then the robot spread his arms wide. He stomped across the bridge. White light shot from his hand. Each time the light hit one of the aliens, they returned to their lizard form and stood still as if frozen.

Luis grinned. His idea was working. His adventure reading had helped him on a real adventure. They would be home in no time!

"Stop!" Zarlok said. He shimmered and

changed, for a moment looking like the captain. But when the robot came toward him, he changed back to his lizard body. He turned and ran past Luis and into the elevator.

White light shot around the room. In moments, the robot had stopped all of the other lizard men. The crew cheered, then quickly returned to their positions.

Luis whispered to Tyler's cat. "The lizard captain escaped."

Uncle Cyrus's voice said, "You must find him. He is the only one who can return the ship's control to you. The ship is not yet safe."

Luis tugged at Casey's arm. "We need to go. Captain Zarlok got away. This isn't over yet."

Casey grabbed Steel and shouted for Tyler. Luis led them into the elevator. Just as the door closed, the ship shook and rattled. From somewhere below, Luis heard an explosion.

A Lying Face

The elevator shook. Lights flickered. Everyone screamed.

"We're running out of time!" Tyler said.

Luis shouted over the sirens blaring in the elevator, "If we don't get this ship under control, we'll have all the time there is . . . to be trapped."

"Elevator, take us back to the last place you stopped," Luis ordered.

"Yes, Captain," the voice said.

Luis paced. They should have taken the alien robot with them. Even if they found Captain Zarlok, could they capture him?

The door opened. Tyler said, "We're back in the engine room. The ship's heart."

"Stop having so much fun," Casey said.

The engine room was louder than before, the machines and engines working too hard. The crew ignored them, running around, shouting, and pressing panels of flashing buttons.

"How will we find him in here?" Luis yelled over the noise.

"We need to separate. This ship is not going to last much longer," Tyler said. He bent toward Steel. "Search for Captain Zarlok."

"Watch out, that lizard could've changed into anyone," Luis warned.

He watched his friends go in different directions. Then he turned and ran back into the elevator and shouted, "Bridge!"

Luis had to get the robot. He was the only thing that could capture Captain Zarlok. Back on the bridge, Luis stepped out and ran right into the red metal beast. "Ouch!"

He glanced at the lizard men. They were still frozen. The crew moved around the bridge. As in the engine room, they shouted at one another as they worked buttons and dials and levers. The warning siren blared and red lights flashed on the walls.

"Robot, come with me," Luis said.

The robot stooped and squeezed into the elevator.

"Engine room!" Luis ordered.

The door opened and he ran out, yelling for the robot to follow him. They moved through the room. Luis had to shout over the noise to assure the frightened crew that the robot was under his control.

He motioned to two men and said, "Stand by the elevator door. Don't let anyone leave."

They nodded and hurried to the elevator.

Luis walked beside the robot and looked behind every machine. He couldn't believe the aliens wanted the ship to blow up. Zarlok said that he and his crew needed it to conquer worlds!

"Hey, over there. Something is moving," Luis said to the robot.

The robot turned and raised an arm. Luis could hear a hum coming from inside the metal body.

"Wait! Don't shoot!"

Tyler stepped from behind a wide machine. "It's just me." He banged a crutch against the robot's leg. "Hey, Metal Man. Good to see you."

Luis said, "Did you see Captain Zarlok?"

Tyler shook his head. "I heard something behind here, but I didn't see anyone. Maybe he slipped out."

Luis pointed toward the elevator. "I set guards at the elevator so no one could leave."

"Have you seen Casey? Or Steel?" Tyler asked.

"No . . . they must still be looking. Maybe we shouldn't have separated," Luis said. "It's dangerous looking for the lizard man without the robot. All Casey could do if she sees him is shout and run away."

Luis turned at a clacking sound. He looked down to see Steel roll against the alien robot's foot. The red robot looked down and blinked at Steel. The cat blinked back several times.

"Must be some kind of robot hello," Tyler said.

Steel rolled over to Luis. "The cat was not able to locate Captain Zarlok. I thought I heard screams, but it must have been the failing engines in this infernal flying machine," Cyrus said.

Luis knew they couldn't give up. They had all the lizard men but one. The most important one. The one who could reset the ship's control.

"Hey, there she is," Tyler said.

Casey ran across the room, breathing hard. "I didn't see anything suspicious," she said. She pointed at the robot, taking a few steps back. "What's he doing here?"

Luis patted the robot. "He's here to help us stop Captain Zarlok when we find him."

Casey said, "Well, he's not here. Let's go back to the bridge."

"Why there?" Tyler asked. "We need to keep searching the rest of the ship."

"No! We should contact the alien ship. Maybe we can make peace. Maybe we can go to their ship and talk," Casey said.

Luis folded his arms. "Are you crazy? We're not getting on that ship. But you're right, we should check the bridge again."

Casey smiled. "Follow me." She turned away and walked past Steel.

The robot cat's tail spun and his ears twisted.

MEOW-BOING! MEORFF-BOING!

Luis said, "Tyler, your cat has gone nuts." He reached for Steel, but it rolled around the alien robot's feet and shouted, "Danger! Danger! A lying face! A lying face!"

Luis looked all around. The crew stopped to stare at them. Could one of them be Zarlok? He said, "Wait, I think he's still here."

Casey stepped toward the elevator. "Don't be ridiculous. We'll lose him if he's gone to the bridge. He'll try to contact his ship."

"Stop," Tyler said. He walked toward his sister. "Where's your jacket?"

"My what?" Casey asked.

Tyler took another step toward her. "Your jacket. With all your pockets of important stuff."

She shrugged. "I must've left it somewhere. It doesn't matter."

Luis stared at his friend. She wouldn't take a million dollars for her jacket full of gadgets. Something was wrong.

Casey moved toward the elevator again. "Well, if you aren't going to the bridge, I'll go by myself."

Luis looked at his friend's eyes. They blinked with scaly eyelids. He shouted, "Tyler, move away from her! Robot, stop her!"

Lizard Casey ran to the elevator. As the door opened, the robot raised his arms. White light shot from them and lit up the elevator as Casey stepped inside.

She shimmered and shook. As she changed into her true form, Captain Zarlok, the elevator door closed.

CHAPTER TEN

TWISTING AGAIN

Luis and Tyler ran to the elevator door. Luis waved a hand over the control panel. Nothing happened.

"Help me get this door open!" he yelled.

Tyler shouted commands to Steel.

The cat rolled across the room. Its legs extended until it was level with the panel. Its metal tongue flicked out and touched the button. Clicks and squeaks went back and forth between the cat and the elevator. Then Steel lowered back to the ground.

"Come on," Luis said. "Open!"

He pounded on the door.

When the door opened, Tyler shouted, "Yes! I knew Steel's tongue would come in handy."

Captain Zarlok stood in the center of the elevator, surrounded by light.

"He's frozen!" Tyler said.

Luis grinned. "We did it. We captured him."

"Yeah, but we have to unfreeze him to get him to give us back control of the ship," Tyler said. Then he yelled at the frozen lizard man, "Where is my sister?"

Luis turned to the giant robot, standing quietly behind them. "Find Casey."

The robot stomped across the room. Luis and Tyler hurried behind him.

In a far corner, behind a tall gray machine, Casey sat on the floor. Her arms were tied. She had a piece of cloth around her mouth.

Tyler pulled the gag from his sister's mouth.

"Ugh," she said. She spat on the ground. "That tastes like lizard."

After untying her, Luis told her what had happened with Captain Zarlok.

A large engine whirred, then stopped. The ship shuddered.

"Sir, the engines are failing!" the chief engineer shouted.

Luis grabbed Steel. "I think this ship is running out of time. Can you hear me, Cyrus?"

"You must get Captain Zarlok to the bridge and unfreeze him," Cyrus said. "Once you leave, the real captain will take care of these aliens."

Everyone squeezed inside the elevator next to the frozen lizard. Luis was sure the robot would crush them if he moved even an inch.

Casey shook her fist at Zarlok. "I'd like to punch you in your lizard nose!"

When the door opened to the bridge, Luis stepped out. The crew saluted him.

"Welcome back, Captain. I see you have captured their leader," the man in gray said.

Luis nodded. The robot carried Captain Zarlok onto the bridge.

Luis took a step toward Zarlok but was thrown to the floor as the ship shook and shuddered.

"Unfreeze him. Now!" Luis ordered.

The alien robot held out his arms again. Light shot toward Zarlok. The lizard blinked, then growled.

"We have your crew," Luis said. "I order you to give me control of this ship again."

Captain Zarlok said, "I will do as you say, but someday, I will have revenge against you, Captain Sanchez."

Luis grinned. "Not me! Maybe your kind will attack another Earth ship one day, but at least I won't ever see your ugly lizard face again."

Luis walked over to the captain's chair, sat down, and leaned over the control panel.

"Robot, bring Captain Zarlok here."

The robot dragged the alien to stand beside Luis's chair.

The whole ship shuddered.

"This thing is going to crack like an egg!" Tyler warned.

Luis shouted, "Okay, lizard man, change control back. Now!"

Captain Zarlok spoke into the computer with his lizard voice. "Computer, this is Captain Zarlok. You will recognize this voice as before."

Lights flashed on the console. "Yes, Captain."

"Return the ship to its previous speed and course."

Luis felt the ship slow. The red alert lights stopped flashing.

Captain Zarlok gave Luis one last glare. His voice changed, now identical to Luis's voice. "Computer, return command to this voice, as well as all previous command voices on this ship."

Casey cheered, "All right! We did it."

Luis smiled. They had completed the adventure.

He said, "Robot, freeze Captain Zarlok until he and his crew are arrested at the space station."

Luis watched the robot drag Captain Zarlok to the other lizard men and freeze him.

As he turned to thank the crew, the room began to spin. He looked at his friends. They were twisting.

He closed his eyes. They were going home.

When the twisting and twirling stopped, Luis opened his eyes. They were in the machine again. He undid his seat belt and jumped up. "We're home!"

Casey grabbed Steel, giving the clunky cat a hug. "I feel like Dorothy in *The Wizard of Oz*. 'There's no place like home!'"

"Uncle Cyrus, are you still there?" Luis asked.

MEOWWW! BOING!

Casey put the cat on the floor. "Maybe Cyrus can only talk to us when we're somewhere in time with the machine."

Luis didn't like thinking about Cyrus lost in time. He had to find a way to rescue him.

Casey twirled around until her jacket clinked and clanked. "We made it home. We rescued Earth in the future. We fought aliens."

Tyler nodded. "We sure did. And now our dads are going to ground us forever. I bet they're wondering where we've been all day."

Luis glanced at the clock across the room. "It's the same time as when we left," he said.

Luis took a deep breath. Their dads would never know. Unless they told them. It wasn't such a bad adventure. Except for the giant robot, the lizard aliens, the ship about to explode, and the chance they might be stuck in time.

"What if we went back in time?" Luis said.

Tyler and Casey grinned.

Luis nodded. Maybe, they could have another adventure. One more couldn't hurt, right?

After all, they had all the time in the world.

HMMM...